BENJAMIN'S THUNDERSTORM

MELANIE FLORENCE   HAWLII PICHETTE

KIDS CAN PRESS

Benjamin loved the rain.

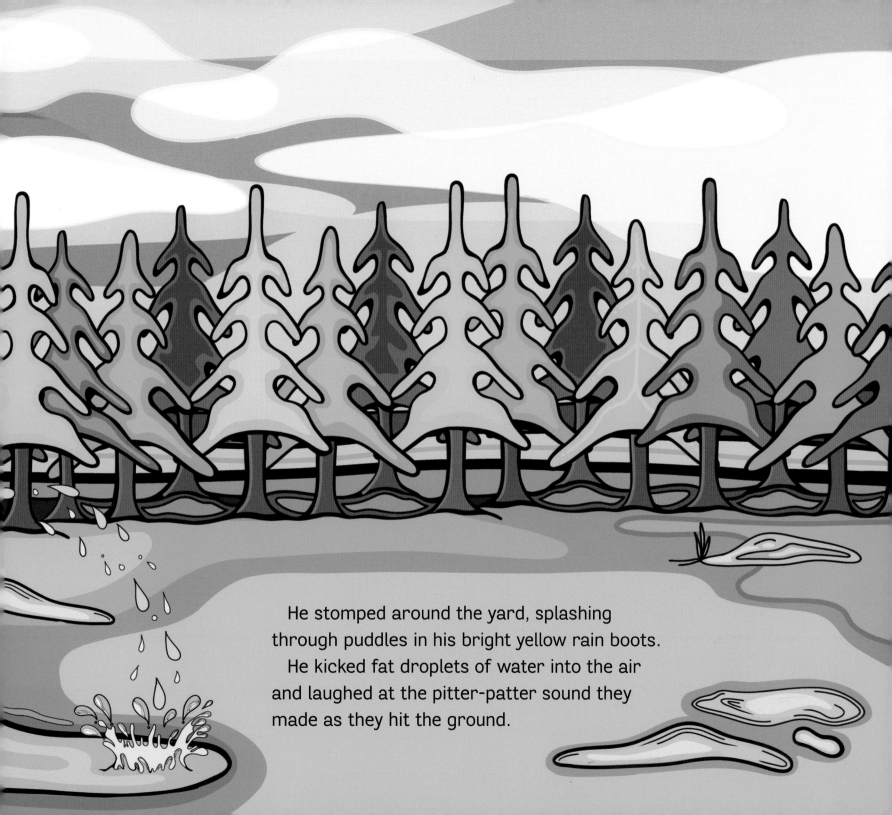

He stomped around the yard, splashing through puddles in his bright yellow rain boots. He kicked fat droplets of water into the air and laughed at the pitter-patter sound they made as they hit the ground.

He jumped high, higher, high as can
be and landed in a puddle as big as a lake.
"Splish, splash, crash," he sang.
"I can make it rain, too."
Thunder growled softly overhead.

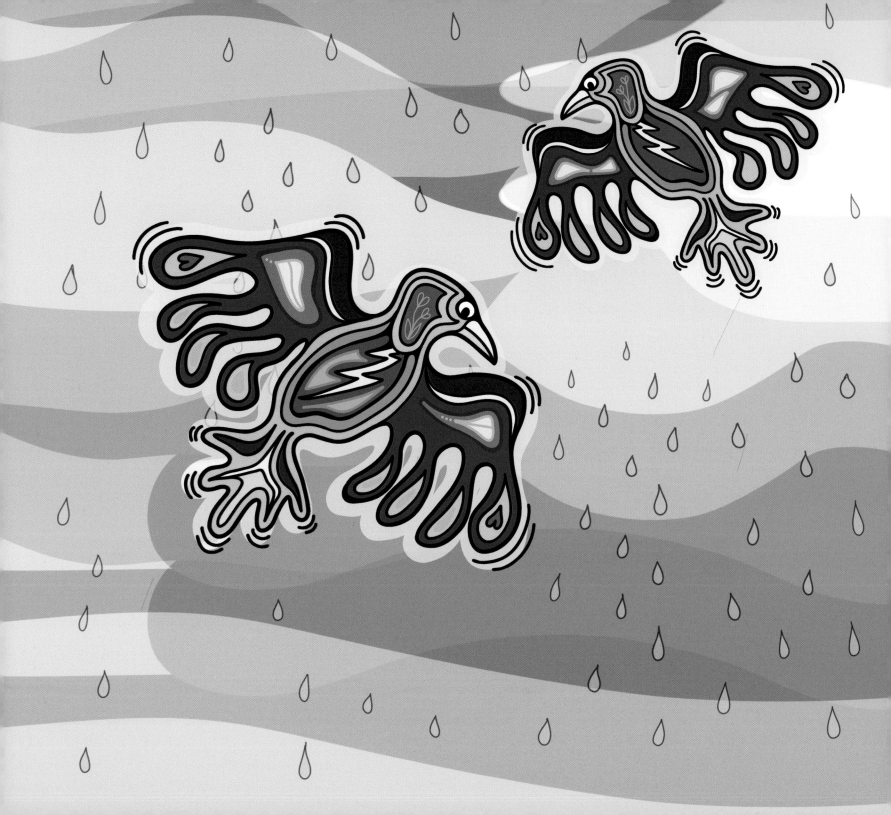

Benjamin loved thunder.

"piyêsiwak!" he rumbled deep in his chest.

His friend Joe told him that thunder was the sound of the thunderbirds beating their giant wings in the sky.

Benjamin thought it sounded exactly like the drum his grandfather played. Like a heartbeat.

"Boom!" roared Benjamin as loud as thunder so piyêsiwak would know that he wasn't afraid.

He stomped into a giant puddle that held a rainbow and watched the colors ripple on the water around his feet.

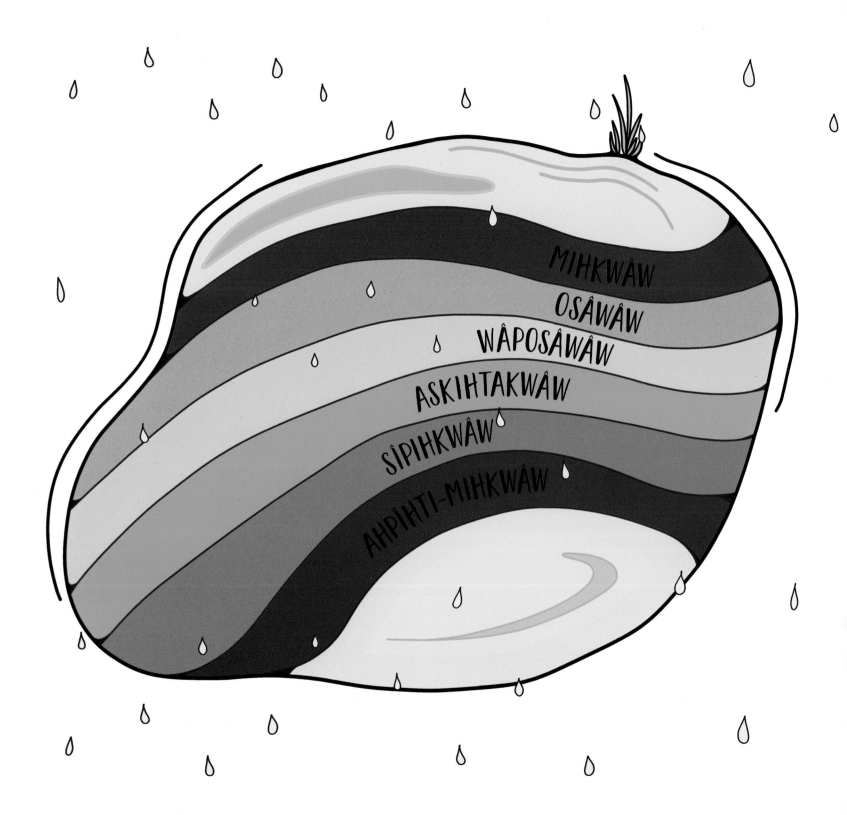

Benjamin liked rainbows. Rainbows and puddles. pîsimoyâpiya êkwa kâ-wâyipêyâsiki. But he loved thunder best.

"piyêsiwak!" Benjamin rumbled again, stomping his feet.
A cracking bolt of lightning shot through the sky, and
Benjamin jumped back.
He didn't like kâ-wâsaskotêpayik at all!

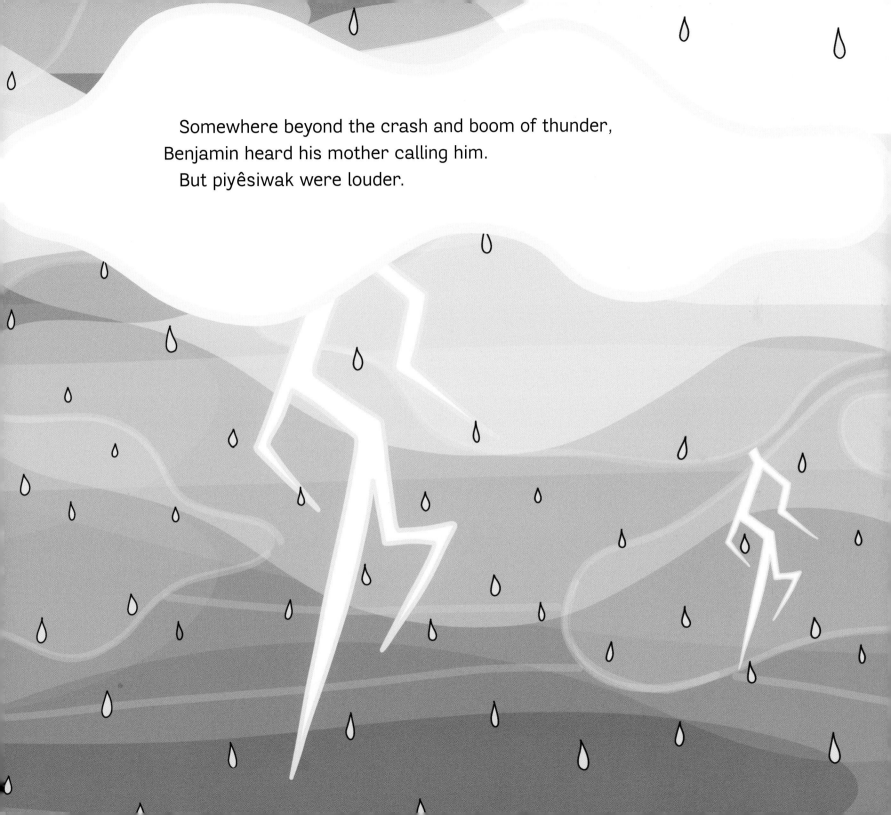

Somewhere beyond the crash and boom of thunder,
Benjamin heard his mother calling him.
But piyêsiwak were louder.

The thunder called to him like the song his grandfather played while his father and the other powwow dancers spun and stepped in time to the drumbeats. And with the sound of thunder rolling through him, Benjamin danced, too.

He danced past puddles, nodding to the rainbows inside them. He spun, first one way, then the other. He tapped his feet and lifted his knees like his father had taught him.

Benjamin spun fast, faster, fast as can be!
And as the sound of thunder stopped, Benjamin
stopped too, holding his pose.

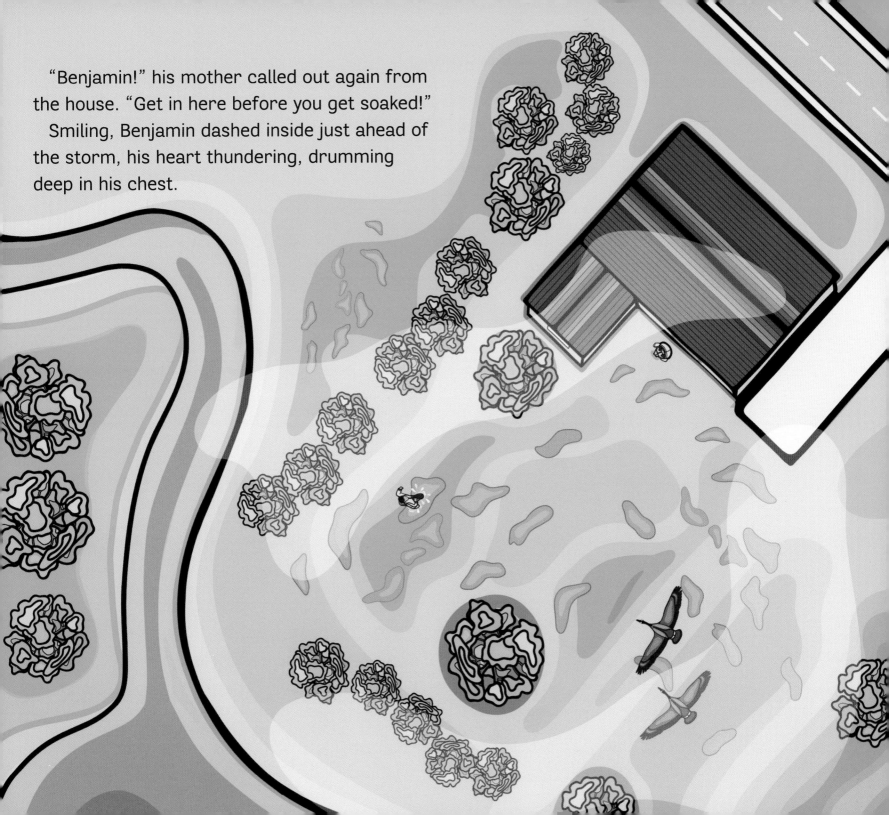

"Benjamin!" his mother called out again from the house. "Get in here before you get soaked!"

Smiling, Benjamin dashed inside just ahead of the storm, his heart thundering, drumming deep in his chest.

Pronunciation Guide

Provided by Dr. Arok Wolvengrey, First Nations University of Canada

The pronunciation guide on this page is an attempt to represent the sounds of Cree using common English spellings (as given within curly brackets {}). Most of the sounds represented are fairly straightforward, but there are still subtleties that cannot be fully captured in writing. Follow these general guidelines:

- {aa} is like English *ah*
- {ow} is meant to sound like the "ow" of English *ow!* or *cow*
- anything spelled {oo} is closer to the "oo" in *book* than the "oo" in *boot*
- the syllable {sew} can vary in sound from something similar to English *sew* to {sih-oo}
- anywhere that "h" occurs in a Cree spelling, it is always pronounced as a breath of air (even before consonants where English speakers are not used to hearing it)

CAPITAL letters represent the main stress (and highest pitch) within a word, and SMALL CAPS represent secondary stress.

ahpîhti-mihkwâw	{uh PEEH TIM meeh KWOW}	"it is purple"
askihtakwâw	{us KEEH tuk KWOW}	"it is green"
êkwa	{ay GWUH}	"and"
kâ-wâsaskotêpayik	{KAA waa SUS koo TAY pie yik}	"lightning"
kâ-wâyipêyâsiki	{kaa WHY yih pay YAA sik kih}	"puddles"
mihkwâw	{meeh KWOW}	"it is red"
osâwâw	{OO sow WOW}	"it is orange"
piyêsiw	{PEE yay SEW}	"thunderbird"
piyêsiwak	{pee YAY sew WUCK}	"thunderbirds"
pîsimoyâpiya	{PEE sim moo YAA pee yuh}	"rainbows"
sîpihkwâw	{SEE peeh KWOW}	"it is blue"
wâposâwâw	{waa POOS sow WOW}	"it is yellow"

For anyone who has ever danced in the rain — M.F.

For my little firebird, Phoenix: you are my greatest inspiration! — H.P.

Text © 2023 Melanie Florence
Illustrations © 2023 Hawlii Pichette

Acknowledgments

Thank you to Dr. Arok Wolvengrey, First Nations University of Canada, for consulting on the Cree words used in this book and creating the pronunciation guide.

Published in Canada and the U.S. by Kids Can Press Ltd.
25 Dockside Drive, Toronto, ON M5A 0B5

Kids Can Press is a Corus Entertainment Inc. company

www.kidscanpress.com

The artwork in this book was rendered digitally.
The text is set in Segaon.

Edited by Yvette Ghione and Kathleen Keenan
Designed by Marie Bartholomew

Printed and bound in Malaysia in 3/2023
by Times Offset

CM 23 0 9 8 7 6 5 4 3 2 1

Library and Archives Canada Cataloguing in Publication

Title: Benjamin's thunderstorm / Melanie Florence ; Hawlii Pichette.
Names: Florence, Melanie, author. | Pichette, Hawlii, illustrator.
Description: Includes some text in Cree.
Identifiers: Canadiana (print) 20220459517 | Canadiana (ebook) 20220459584 | ISBN 9781525303203 (hardcover) | ISBN 9781525310768 (EPUB)
Subjects: LCGFT: Picture books. | LCGFT: Fiction.
Classification: LCC PS8611.L668 B46 2023 | DDC jC813/.6 — dc23

Kids Can Press gratefully acknowledges that the land on which our office is located is the traditional territory of many nations, including the Mississaugas of the Credit, the Anishnabeg, the Chippewa, the Haudenosaunee and the Wendat peoples, and is now home to many diverse First Nations, Inuit and Métis peoples.

We thank the Government of Ontario, through Ontario Creates; the Ontario Arts Council; the Canada Council for the Arts; and the Government of Canada for supporting our publishing activity.